UNDER the Table

What a young woman will do for money.

Sitting all alone on the expensive sofa in the lavish dining room, Jess Hall hugged herself as nervous butterflies flittered around her belly. She still wasn't sure that she could go through with what was expected of her. She glanced up at the ornate grandfather clock to see that she only had fifteen more minutes before the guests were going to arrive. Looking over to the huge dining table that took up the better part of the room, she tried to picture what it was going to be like. She wanted to go home, just walk out past the grey haired butler and swing open the heavy double doors that led to the stone walkway and the driveway beyond.

What kept her from leaving though was the fact that her home would not be her home much longer if she didn't find a way to make some money quick. She was at this point three months behind on her rent and had been given until Friday to pay up or move out. Tomorrow was Friday and there was no other option. If she lost her place, she would be forced to move back in with her parents and that was even a worse option than what she was facing tonight. The irony about all this was that her parents were rich business people who could and would help her out if she asked, but it was the way they would make her feel about asking that had her so adamant about doing it on her own.

She also had an older sister and brother-in-law who were lawyers and would help her out too, but asking them for help was worse than asking her folks. As for the rest of her family, she had an aunt and uncle that was close, but they had already raised two kids who had moved on and they weren't rich. Her two cousins were young like Jess and they were struggling also.

Jess was twenty years old and she had made many mistakes in her life. Probably the worst mistake she had made was not finishing college. It was unheard of that she wouldn't finish college and her parents were so upset when she quit, especially since they were paying for it. But she was so sure that college was just not what she wanted. She was sick of school and she was ready to start her life, no matter what challenges she came up against. Determination was her strong suit and she was sure that she knew everything that she needed to know to thrive. Her trust fund of one hundred thousand dollars would get her started and she would move on from there. No worries.

That was two years ago and things just hadn't gone the way she had expected. The money was all gone and the jobs that she was sure she would get just didn't last and now she was broke and scared. Her latest job as a waitress, she had kept for just two months and it was the most difficult that she had had. On her last day when her boss fired her for screwing up yet again, she was met on the way out by one of her only repeat customers. An older woman named Barbara West who was always dressed in designer clothes and left large tips.

Seeing that Jess was upset, Barbara asked what the problem was. When she heard the news, she showed genuine concern and asked what kind of work that she would be interested in doing.

"Oh, at this point, I would do anything." was her answer.

Barbara smiled and said "Well dear, I just might be able to help you out after all." She reached into her designer purse and pulled out a pad of paper and a gold pen. Jess wondered what she was doing as she watched her write something on the top sheet and rip it off. "This is my address. Be at my house tonight at six o-clock sharp if you want to make enough money to get your rent caught up and still have more left over."

"What kind of work are you talking about?" Jess asked, wondering how one night of work could earn her enough to pay three months' rent and still have money left over.

"All I can tell you now is that it is a service job, and I pay very well if I think you're worth it. I'll leave it up to you; if you show up at six, the job is yours. Think about it."

This was very confusing to Jess "You'll give me the job if I show up? What if I don't have any experience?"

Barbara smiled "Don't worry hon, anyone can do this job. Besides, you've been serving me for months here, I already know you'll be perfect for the job."

With that she went into the restaurant leaving Jess standing on the stoop.

Five hours later she knocked loudly on the large double doors of the huge mansion wondering just what kind of work she would be doing. A fifty-ish balding man opened the doors and asked "Can I help you miss?"

Jess smiled and said "Hello, I'm Jessica Hall. Mrs. West told me to be here at six o-clock for a job."

The butler nodded and stepped to the side to let her in. As she walked past him, he said "Madam West is not married miss Hall. She prefers to be addressed as madam or mistress."

"Oh okay, thank you." she said as she let him lead the way past a grand staircase to an office.

"Have a seat miss Hall, Madam West will be in shortly."

Jess walked into the room and sat in the comfortable leather chair. Two minutes later Barbara West walked in, her high heel shoes clomping across the wood floor. "Jessica, I'm so glad that you showed up." Jess stood up and started to speak but was cut off "We have very little time to waste so follow me and I will explain." She headed back the way she came and Jess quickly followed.

Out in the hall Barbara kept talking. "At seven

o-clock this evening, I have several guests coming over for dinner and extras. This is not your average dinner party though, these guests are all high power people. They are the movers and shakers of this state and they all are under tremendous pressure with their careers. Therefore, when they come here for a party, they expect a little more than usual."

If this was supposed to clear things up for Jess, it wasn't. She decided to interrupt. "So what will my job be?" She asked, almost running to keep up.

"I'm getting to that." They walked into a large dining room and that was when Jess saw the huge table for the first time. It was immense and covered with a very dark heavy table cloth that drooped down to the seats of the chairs.

"This is where the guests will be served their food," she paused for a moment before adding, "and serviced by you."

"Oh, you want me to wait on them."

Barbara smiled and shook her head "No Jess, I have wait staff that will take care of that."

"Well then, what do you need me for?" This was so confusing.

"I want you to service them Jess, orally."

It took a three count before it clicked in her head exactly what she meant, and then Jess gasped in shock and stepped back. "You...you want me to..." she was shaking her head and her eyes were as wide as saucers. "I can't do that ma'am."

"You can do it Jess, and from what you told me today at the restaurant, you need the money too much to refuse."

"But...how much money are you talking about." she couldn't even believe that she was able to ask that question because her face had seemingly gone numb, along with most of her body.

"If you can satisfy all my guests, you will earn five thousand dollars."

This was all too much to take in for Jess who had very little experience with sex. She had been with two guys and she was drunk with the first one. The second guy she sucked him for all of two minutes, then let him fuck her. "I don't know, isn't it illegal. I mean it's prostitution."

"Honey, you don't have to worry about that. The guests that come here are rich and famous people. If it ever got out that they were coming here for sex with a stranger, their careers would be toast. They pay extra to ensure discretion and I have gone to great lengths to keep their confidentiality intact. My guests come from all walks of life. Doctors, politicians, lawyers, actors, judges, even high ranking military personnel. They all have one thing in common, they are rich. I'm the only one who knows who they are and I'm not telling."

"Wouldn't I know who they were if I agree to this?" it was a reasonable question, after all she was supposed to service these guys orally. In her mind they had to all be guys, even though she had only been told 'guests' .

"You wouldn't see them and they wouldn't see you. The way it works is, you get under that table before the guests are shown in. They will all be wearing masks on their faces so they won't be seen even if you do peek. I supply them robes so their top half is covered, but their bottom half is easily accessible by you. Once they are seated at the table, you won't be able to see anything above their waist, so they are free to remove the masks if they so choose. There are two rules for you. First, there is no talking at all by you. They do not want to hear you, even though they all know that there is a pretty young lady beneath the table, they don't want to be reminded of it while they are eating. Second, you must not attempt to see who is at the table, no matter what. So if you have any plans at all about trying to blackmail or contacting the press to try to cash in, don't do it. Remember what I said about these people. They can and will make your life much more miserable than you could make theirs."

"When you have finished pleasuring each guest, and they have all finished their meals, I will lead them all out of the dining room and you will come out from under the table. I will send my butler in with your payment, and you will be free to go."

Jess took a deep breath and swallowed hard, then she looked around the room once more. She was trying to convince herself that she could do this. It was not easy because she knew that she shouldn't but the money was just too good to pass up. She saw no other alternative. She looked back at Barbara and nodded slowly, almost imperceptibly. "Okay, I need the money." she whispered.

"Of course you do dear, I wouldn't have asked

you here if you didn't. Now, don't forget the rules, it is very important, especially if you want to be invited back." She was standing beside one of the chairs and she pulled it out. "As you can see, each chair is specially made for easy access." the chair seats were made short with a curved edge to allow oral sex. "You have time to sit down and relax for a few minutes, but you must crawl under the table and pull the chair back by ten of seven, no later. Is that clear?"

Jess nodded and said "Yes ma'am. I'll do my best."

"Very well. I must go get ready to receive my guests." With that she left the room and closed the heavy door behind her.

At ten of seven, Jess got up on shaky legs and made her way over to the chair that was still pulled out. She peered under the table and saw that it was quite dark. Thinking that it might make it easier for her to do if she couldn't see much. She got down on her hands and knees and crawled under, then turned and pulled the chair back in behind her. Once the chair was pulled in there was even less light and she backed up to the head of the table.

The room was quiet for another five minutes before the door opened and she could hear several people walking across the floor toward the table. Jess was shivering but she wasn't cold, she was nervous. As chairs were pulled out she could see flashes of light and several sets of legs covered by the bottom half of robes slid into the chairs and the light was blocked again.

Jess sat in the middle of the table afraid to touch anybody and looking around. She realized with dawning horror that out of the eight people who were here, five were women and three were men. The men wore blue robes whole the women wore pink. She hadn't thought that there would be women here. She wanted to get out of here and she could go to the end chair which was unoccupied, but she was afraid. There was talking above her but it was muted and she figured that it was the table blocking the sound.

Realizing that she wasn't getting anywhere by just sitting here and her bills wouldn't be paid if she wasn't paid, she slid over to the nearest man and, with trembling hands, she opened his robe and looked at his flaccid penis. It was curled around his hairless nut sack, looking like a fat worm. She stared at it for a few moments, inspecting it and not daring to touch it yet. She didn't notice his hands moving around her until she felt her hair grabbed and suddenly she was pulled forward roughly, her nose flattened against his soft cock.

The smell of his sex was not entirely unpleasant, but it was strong and it filled her nostrils as she tried to pull her head back. He didn't let go and she felt his manhood swelling as it filled with blood. Her hands were on his thighs and she took a few moments before she realized that this was what she was here for.

Tentatively she stuck out her tongue and licked back and forth on the base of his suddenly throbbing seven inch cock. She started to slide her tongue up the length of his rod, but only made it about half way before he pushed her back down. At first she was confused. She was expecting to give him head and from what she knew about giving head, that meant sucking the 'head' of his penis. Instead, he pushed her down until her mouth was on his ball sack.

She wasn't sure what he wanted until he started pushing his crotch up into her face and tilting himself, opening his legs wide and exposing himself more to her. She stuck her tongue out again and licked around his nut sack, realizing for the first time that they were completely hairless. He moved one hand to the top of her head and the other moved down by her mouth. She felt and tasted his fingers momentarily as he grabbed one of his balls through his scrotum and lifted it, pushing it toward her lips.

She understood at that point that he wanted her to suck on his balls so she opened her mouth wide and engulfed his testicle. It was way larger than she expected it to be and at first it slipped out, leaving her with a mouthful of his scrotum skin. He moved quickly though pulling his nut back up and inserting it back into her mouth. This time she sucked and closed her lips around the bulbous ball. She heard a muffled moan from above and his hands pulled away from her. She was encouraged by his movements and continued suckling and twirling her tongue around.

She had never done this before. Sure she had sucked one cock for a few minutes, but sucking balls was different. It wasn't bad, just like sucking that other guys cock hadn't been that bad either, just different. She sucked the one testicle for about thirty seconds before wondering if she could get both in her mouth at the same time. She moved her hand up and started working his other one in, opening her mouth as wide as she could. She knew how easy it was to hurt a man's testicles and she didn't want to hurt this man.

She didn't know who it was but she sensed that hurting him would not be good for her cause. At the same time, she knew if he enjoyed having one nut in her mouth, then two would be better. It was a stretch but she finally managed to slip the other one in. Her mouth was impossibly full with the spongy mass and her tongue fit nicely between the two oblong balls. She wiggled her tongue around and felt him tense up.

Saliva had pooled in the bottom of her mouth and started to drool out and down her chin. Attempting to slurp up the drool, she slid her tongue over her bottom lip and under his fleshy scrotum. She heard him groan and then thought she heard him saying something about " Oh yeah lick my ass" or something close. That was when she realized, how close she was to actually doing that. She wasn't actually licking his ass but she was licking the skin beneath his balls which was very close to his asshole.

It kind of wigged her out a bit, especially because she didn't know who this man was. She was looking up at his swollen penis waving in front of her eyes. Even though there was little light down here, her eyes had adjusted and she could see a drop of clear liquid slowly drip down the head of his member. She knew that it was pre-cum and that meant that he was close to orgasm. She pushed with her tongue, popping his balls out of her stretched mouth and moving with more confidence now, she put his cock head in her mouth.

His head was throbbing and hot and her wet mouth slid down past the helmet till she felt him in the back of her mouth. She could not deep throat so she wrapped her hand around the base and moved her mouth up and down, sucking and twirling her tongue around. She knew he must be close, but she didn't know how close until he grabbed her head and held her while he erupted his boiling seed into her throat. It surprised her so much that she tried to pull back but he held her tight.

It was her first taste of sperm and she really didn't like it one bit but she couldn't pull back and her mouth was soon filled to overflowing. Not knowing what to do in the moment, she swallowed the bitter tasting sludge down and felt it coating her throat and warming her all the way down to her belly. After six squirts he finally let her go and she sat back on her heels, wiping her mouth with the back of her hand.

Her mouth was filled with the terrible taste of sperm and she worried that the next man would do the same, forcing her to swallow. She looked across the table at the woman sitting opposite of the man she just took care of. She was scared to perform oral sex on a woman, but she couldn't do another man right now. She slid over and without hesitating (she may have changed her mind had she hesitated) she opened the robe and looked at the pussy.

It appeared to be a young woman. Her skin was so soft and smooth and her pussy lips were thin. She was also hairless. She leaned in rather close and inhaled the smell of the pussy. It was not at all unlike her own smell (which she secretly enjoyed). The owner of this pussy readjusted her bottom on the chair, sliding her butt forward as far as she could without falling off the narrow seat and spreading her legs wide. This movement caused her labia to spread open, revealing a wonderful pink gash and a slightly stronger smell. As much as she didn't want to admit it, the smell was kind of intoxicating and Jess noticed a familiar tingle in her own pussy that she hadn't felt when she sucked the penis.

A small delicate hand slid under the table and found Jess's cheek. The gentle hand caressed the side of her face and her thumb slid down to her lips. Her breath caught in her throat as she felt the thumb glide softly over her lips and carefully pull down her bottom lip. She let the strange unknown woman slide her thumb into her mouth and she closed her lips on the digit and sucked. It was amazingly erotic and Jess's hand slid up the woman's smooth thigh. Her fingers came to rest on the inner thigh, right next to her plumping labia, but she didn't touch her pussy yet.

The hand on her face pulled away and landed on the pussy in front of her. She watched fascinated as the first two fingers rubbed up and down then spread open the lips, revealing her clitoris. Jess was so enthralled with the show in front of her eyes that she didn't see the girls other hand reach under and grab her head from the other side. She wasn't rough at all, not like the man had been. In fact, there was almost a loving way that she gently found the back of Jess's head and pulled her forward.

Jess understood that the girl was horny and she let herself be pulled forward until her lips came into contact with the delicate pussy lips.

She wasn't afraid anymore of tasting a woman and she opened her mouth and licked up the length of the moist slit. She heard a faint feminine moan from above and she went to work. Being that this was the very first time that she had ever gone down on a woman, she figured that she would do what felt good to her. Although she had let two guys fuck her, only one had attempted to go down on her and he had been clumsy and too rough. His whiskers had pricked her sensitive skin and after only about thirty seconds of him slurping around, she pulled him up to fuck. It hadn't been very pleasant.

She started down low, at the very bottom of the pussy hole and she licked carefully and slowly around the opening. The taste was about what she thought it would be as she had tasted her own juices before. It was rather pleasant and she was getting more and more turned on the longer her face was here. After she licked all around and inside, she slowly slid her tongue up through the now engorged labial lips. When she reached the clit, she first licked all around it before flicking it with the tip of her tongue and then wrapping her lips around the tiny clit and sucking it.

She must have been doing something right because she felt the thighs tighten as the legs closed on both sides of her head. Realizing that this girl was on her way to an orgasm, Jess renewed flicking her tongue while her lips were still wrapped around the clit and she was gently sucking.

She wished she could see this woman's face, but that was impossible. She could imagine it though and she pictured her as a pretty brunette, maybe with her hair tied back and wearing glasses for that librarian look. She imagined her face flushed red and her eyes narrowed to small slits. Her lips would be a rich shade of red and opened in an 'O' shape as she tilted her head back. Her hands and toes would be clenching along with her puckered asshole as she was pushed closer and closer to the edge.

As Jess was painting this picture in her head, she had slid her own hand down between her legs and was rubbing her own pussy through her pants. The pussy at her mouth, the pussy attached to a woman she didn't know and would never see, started to clench and she heard a loud but somewhat muffled "OOOOOOHHHHHHH". Suddenly, the woman who was cumming started bouncing her pussy around as her clitoris became super sensitive to the wildly flicking tongue and sucking lips that were still working their magic.

For a moment, Jess tried to stay with her as she didn't want to stop sucking and licking, but then she realized what was happening and she slid down to the now very wet pussy that was still locked in spasms. The bouncing stopped as she slid her tongue back into the now clenching opening. The juices now tasted different, thicker and muskier and it turned Jess on even more.

She continued to gently lap around the pussy until the young lady pushed her away. As she sat back on her heels, she looked at the pussy that she had just finished pleasing and was amazed at how different it looked now from before she started to lick. For one thing, it was much redder and plumper. The lips were splayed out and wet with a thick white creamy cum. Where before it looked so tight and neat, now it was spread open and dishevelled. It was an amazing sight and she wished she could spend more time on this one pussy, but she had so many more people to deal with that she reluctantly pulled away, letting her hand slide down her soft thigh and off her knee.

She looked around once again and decided that she could do another woman before finishing the next guy. She sidled over to the next pink robe and confidently opened it to reveal the next pussy. It was an overweight woman with a strong smell. She pulled back as the smell assaulted her nostrils and had to calm her suddenly nervous stomach. She tentatively sniffed and realized that the smell wasn't as bad as she first thought. Sure it was a much thicker and heavier smell than the first pussy she smelled and tasted, but it really wasn't that bad.

This woman's legs were as thick around as Jess's waist and her belly rolls hung partway over her crotch. She was also hairy and where the first pussy had been so neat looking before she started, this pussy looked rather forbidding.

Jess truly had nothing against fat people, in fact, she had an aunt that was always struggling with her weight and was probably as big as this woman, if not bigger. She loved her aunt and was very close to her.

Steeling herself for what she expected to be a difficult task, Jess leaned in close and tried to lick the plump pussy. Her forehead however, pressed up against the flabby belly and the way she was kneeling made it nearly impossible for her to reach without straining her neck. She tried turning her head but was met on both sides by the thick thighs.

As if realizing that she was having trouble, the woman wiggled her large ass forward to the edge of the seat and using one hand, she pulled up her belly, giving Jess the room she needed.

Thinking over and over 'I need the money. I need the money' Jess closed her eyes and lunged forward. Her nose got in the way at first and sunk into the moist flesh. She pushed herself onward and started licking. The taste was far different from the first pussy. This had a saltier taste which she figured was probably sweat. It was also very creamy and it coated her tongue. She wasted little time and quickly went after the clitoris, which was much more pronounced than the first. This one stuck out nearly an inch and she sucked it into her mouth like a mini cock.

She felt the large body shudder as she flicked her tongue back and forth on the swelling nub. Hoping it would help, she slid her hand beneath her chin and slid two fingers into the cunt as deep as she could. It was soft, wet and very warm and she pushed on the upper wall as she slid her fingers in and out. Form above she could hear someone huffing over and over like an old steam engine train.

She could feel juices running down her hand as she fingered faster. She could also feel the massive legs on either side of her face twitching and trembling. Sensing that orgasm was close, Jess took a chance and tried pushing all four fingers into the sloppy pussy. She was surprised when they slid in rather easily and she pushed her hand in all the way to her thumb.

That turned out to be the trigger that set her off and suddenly Jess found herself clamped tightly between those thunderous thighs. If her ears hadn't been completely sealed she would have heard screaming and "I'm cccccuuuuuummmmmmmiiinnnngggg" and a few other grunts and groans. She didn't hear a thing though other than her own heartbeat in her head. She also heard and felt a powerful spray of hot liquid that squirted over her hand, hitting her neck and running down her chest.

Wedged between the giant legs she was unable to pull back as she felt what she thought was pee spray her and soak her blouse. She couldn't even pull her lips off the woman's clit or her hand from her pussy until finally the cellulite laden thighs loosened up. Jess pulled away as soon as she could.

For a split second she almost fled the scene. There were two empty chairs on either end of the table that she could easily push out and she could run from the room without looking back. Thinking that she had been pissed on, especially so close to her mouth, had really unsettled her and had her second guessing her decision. But when she looked down at the small puddle on the floor, she saw that the liquid was clear instead of yellow. She also could smell the fluid and although it had a strong odour, it was not the smell of piss. Jess may have been young, but she was aware that some women could ejaculate just like men when they came and that was what it appeared had happened. It made her feel good that she had caused this woman to cum so hard that she squirted.

What she didn't like though was having a big wet sticky mess on her shirt. Knowing that the people at the table were not going to look under the table, she pulled her top off and dropped it on the floor. Realizing that her bra was wet too, she slipped out of that also.

Topless now, she moved over to the next blue robe and opened it with her wet hand. A seven inch uncut penis popped up, standing straight up. She giggled under her breath and realized that up top it must be very erotic to see people next to yourself moaning in orgasm but not being able to see what's going on underneath. They could only imagine what was going on and anticipate what was going to happen to them. She was really starting to get into this now.

This was the first uncircumcised penis that she had ever seen in person and she wanted to examine it. She reached up and cupped his balls with her left hand while she used just the tips of her fingers on her right hand to play with his foreskin. Pulling the skin down to expose the head, then sliding it back up. The cock twitched and some pre-cum oozed out of the slit. It seemed that it wouldn't take much manipulation to make this one erupt.

Leaning in she extended her tongue and licked up the shaft. She used her hand to pull the foreskin down, then tickled the slit with the tip of her tongue. She pulled back for a moment and saw that his cock head was turning purple. She moved in quickly and engulfed the head with her lips, not to suck but to tease and make it wet. She barely touched him with her lips, simply encircled the head and drooled a dollop of saliva down the side of his throbbing prick. As the spit dripped down, she slid up so her breasts were on either side of his cock and used her hands to trap him between them.

It was awkward and cramped and she had to keep her head tilted down to fit which put her mouth right at the top of his cock. She could barely move at all but she didn't need to. Lifting up and down as much as she possibly could she felt his manhood sliding in between her mounds and with her lips covering his cock head, she sucked and licked all around his pee slit until she felt the head expanding even bigger before the first hot blast of semen squirted over her tongue.

She pulled back this time but kept stroking with her hand while he spewed all over his belly. She stroked him until there was no more sperm leaking from the tip of his cock and he started to lose his erection.

Four were done and four remained and Jess wanted to do another woman. She moved back across the table to the next pink robe and opened it. It was a surprise to see that this woman was black. Jess was not prejudice at all, in fact she had a relative who was black. Her aunt had adopted a black girl fifteen years ago named Dianna who had grown up with Jess. Di, as she liked to be called, was now twenty years old and beautiful and living with a white woman.

Now, as Jess stared into the dark pussy in front of her, she briefly wondered if it would taste the same as the young white pussy she ate first. This pussy also belonged to a young woman and from the appearance, it seemed that the owner was already turned on. She guessed that because there was clear fluid already seeping out. She leaned in close, putting her nose right up to the hairless pubic area, and breathed deeply, savouring the smell. She could smell a familiar scent of perfume but couldn't place it.

She stuck out her tongue and pushed it deeply between the pussy lips of the black woman eliciting a strong moan from above her. She thought it was kind of funny that the voice of the moan sounded just a little bit like her cousin. She delved on, pushing her tongue as deeply as she could and tasting the excitement of the unknown young black lady. She was playing a game in her head of imagining what each person looked like by what their sexual organs looked like. This pussy in her mind belonged to a pretty young woman who looked a little like Halle Barry but with darker skin. This woman had skin as dark as Ti, or so it seemed. It was hard to tell how dark her skin was because of the low light.

The taste of this pussy wasn't at all like either of the other ones she had already licked, but it still tasted lovely. She stayed with her tongue in deep for several seconds then slid it out and licked up between the inner pussy lips. When she reached the clit she heard another moan and once again smiled at the way it sounded like her cousin. She worked quickly tickling with her tongue and sucking with her lips. Her fingers found the hole that her tongue had just vacated and she slid her first two digits in deep.

She had to tilt her head to the side a bit with her hand where it was but it wasn't too uncomfortable. With her fingers buried deep she could gauge how close this woman was to cumming by the way her pussy clenched and unclenched. With each clench, her fingers were squeezed and more fluid dripped out. It took all of three minutes licking and fingering before her fingers were squeezed much tighter. She could tell that she was bringing on another orgasm.

Jess herself was more horny than she had ever been and really wanted to masturbate but she still had three more people to finish off before she would get paid. She wondered what course was being served up top and how much longer she had to finish. With one more man and two more women, she decided to finish the man first and end with back to back pussies.

She backed away from the black lady and was impressed by how much her legs were shaking as she experienced the fading effects of her orgasm. Quickly she slid back across the table to the last blue robe that hadn't been opened. She half expected the man to be black but when she opened the robe it was another white man. This one was circumcised and this one was the longest of the three. He was semi hard and he was seven inches long. Once he felt his robe being opened though, his cock grew quickly without her even touching it. Once he was fully erect he was nine inches long but very thin. The head was quite large and shaped rather like a mushroom and the shaft was lined with thick veins that stood out nearly a quarter inch.

She pushed his now erect penis up until it was laying on his belly and she went down on his balls. If the first guy liked it so much she figured this guy probably would also. She put her lips against his sack which was covered in short stubble that was remarkably soft, and sucked in a mouthful of his scrotum. His right testicle popped into her open mouth and she closed her lips around it as much as she could without putting too much pressure on it.

Once again she heard a loud but muffled "UUUUUHHHH" sound over her head and she knew that he liked it. She had a hold of his penis in her hand and she wrapped her fingers tightly around the shaft. She stroked up and down while she lavished his testicle in her mouth. His prick was jumping in her hand and she figured that he was real close so she popped her mouth off his now spit covered ball sack and she quickly engulfed his cock head. She couldn't raise her head up much because of the table so she kept stroking with her hands and just sucked like a vacuum cleaner.

His hands came down on both sides of her head and they were balled into fists. She worried that he was going to grab her head like the first guy did but he didn't touch her. Instead, he just started squirting without warning. The first hot spray surprised her and she pulled up too quick, thumping her head hard on the bottom of the table and for a moment she saw stars. Her mouth though was still full of his cock head and while she was dazed he was still shooting sperm into her mouth.

Then he thrust up, his cock entering the back

of her throat, and she gagged and nearly threw up. She somehow managed to breathe through her nose and fight the urge to puke as his cock leaked more sperm. She slid back letting his still creaming prick slide out of her mouth and rubbed the lump on the back of her head. Her mouth was still full of cum and she swallowed with a grimace then wiped her mouth with the back of her hand.

There were two more to go and they were both female. The last two ladies were sitting next to each other on the other side of the table and Jess sidled over between the two. Her mouth and tongue were tired and she wanted to hurry things along so she decided to try something a little different. Sitting between both ladies, she used both hands to open both robes at the same time. Both of them looked to be more mature ladies from the looks of things. She guessed that they were both at least in there forties and one was probably older than that.

It really didn't matter to her how old they were, she had come this far and she wasn't going to stop now with only two left. She slid both hands up the insides of both ladies thighs and started fingering them both. They were both very moist but she thought they could each use some more lubrication so she pulled her hands back and spit in both. She rubbed the spit into their cunts and started working on them both. That was when she noticed that each one had her hand down by her side and she got another idea. She reached over and grabbed both of their hands and crossed them over to each other's cunts.

It was a risky move to be sure but she was feeling more daring than usual. At first neither one made any move and she thought that she had fucked up good. 'Oh well' she thought and she pushed on both of their fingers, driving them into the wet pussies. Then something remarkable happened and they both started to finger fuck each other. Jess sat back and watched for about ten seconds as they both drove their fingers in and out of their pussies. She probably could have just sat back and watched the show and let them pleasure each other because they both seemed to be enjoying it, but she wanted to help.

She put her hands back and started rubbing all around both of their crotches. They were both soaked by now and they were both into fingering each other so she made sure her fingers were plenty wet and she stuck both of her middle fingers into each woman's ass hole. They were much tighter than the pussies and now she understood why guys liked to fuck girls assholes so much.

She pushed her two fingers in and out of the two ladies asses and could feel them each pulsating and clenching. Both women were heavily leaking from their pussies which lubricated her fingers enough. Her hands were curled into fists except for her middle fingers and she punched and pulled, punched and pulled until they both started to cum at the same time. It was amazing to watch these two pussies side by side as they both started to jump around as they rode the waves of pleasure to the end.

Finally she slid her two fingers out of their asses and sat back. She was finished and she only needed to wait for them to all leave. It took another five minutes or so before they all started to get up and push their chairs back in. a few minutes later the room was empty and she climbed out and stood up, stretching her body which had been cooped up for so long. She carried her bra and shirt in her hand. They were still wet and the room was empty so she wasn't worried. She sat on the couch and put on her damp clothes and waited.

About ten minutes later, the butler came in and placed an envelope in her hand.

She opened it and pulled out a piece of paper that read - Congratulations Jessica, my guests have enjoyed your talents very much. Your payment of five thousand dollars cash is here. They have all raved about how good you were at pleasing them and they would like to schedule another dinner with you under the table again. The choice ultimately is yours, so think about it and I will be calling you in a few days to find out your answer."

It was signed with just a big flourishing letter B.

She took out the money, counted it, folded it and put it in her pocket. She turned to the butler who motioned for her to follow him and he led her to the front door, happy that she had money to pay her bills and a way to earn more soon.

If you enjoyed the story look at my other stories:

https://www.amazon.com/dp/B08XQVBMKR

www.ingramcontent.com/pod-product-compliance
Lightning Source LLC
Chambersburg PA
CBHW071243140726
47996CB00007B/2732